Produced by Kroha Associates, Inc.
Middletown, Connecticut.

Printed in the United States of America.

ISBN 1-56326-113-8

Best Friends Forever

One sunny day, Minnie and Daisy were walking home from the shopping mall wearing the new best-friend bracelets they had just bought. Each bracelet had a half-a-heart charm on it. The girls held their arms out to watch the charms shine in the sun.

"These bracelets are very special," said Minnie. "I love that when we put our charms together, they make a whole heart, and they spell out the words, 'best friends.'"

"That's us, all right!" Daisy said, smiling.

Suddenly, a girl with bouncy brown ponytails skipped up to them from the yard next to Minnie's house.

"Hi!" she said. "I'm Julie. You must be Minnie. My grandma told me lots of nice things about you!"

"Hi, Julie! I'm glad to meet you," said Minnie. "This is my best friend, Daisy."

Daisy smiled shyly. "Do you live here now?" she asked.

"Oh, no! I'm just visiting my grandma for a month," Julie explained.

"Visiting my grandma is always fun," Julie said. "But it would be even nicer with some friends my own age to play with. Do you want to play dolls?"

"That sounds great!" Minnie said. "Come on, Daisy."

"I can't play now," Daisy answered. "I promised I'd go straight home from the mall. I'll see you tomorrow, Minnie. It was nice to meet you, Julie," she said.

As she waved good-bye, Daisy's bracelet jingled on her arm.

" 'Bye, Daisy!" Minnie and Julie called together.

"Let's make doll dresses," Julie suggested. She showed Minnie a big basket full of fabric. "My grandma gave me all these scraps," she said. "We can use anything we want."

"I like this," Minnie said, taking out some polka-dotted fabric.

"This is my favorite!" Julie said as she held up a piece of material with tiny flowers on it.

Soon they were both sewing busily and talking like old friends.

Julie's lots of fun to play with, Minnie thought. *She's really good at making doll clothes!*

The next day, Daisy and Minnie were riding bikes when Julie came over.

"Want to ride bikes with us?" Minnie asked.

"Sure, but I don't have a bike here," sighed Julie.

"Share mine!" Minnie exclaimed, hopping off her bicycle.

"Gee, thanks," said Julie. "I know — let's make an obstacle course!" Minnie and Julie put lawn chairs in the driveway and took turns riding between them.

"I'm a circus clown riding on a tightrope," Julie shouted. She wobbled and wiggled on Minnie's bike.

Minnie laughed but Daisy didn't. "I'm tired of bike riding," Daisy said. "I'm going home."

All that week, Minnie and Julie played together. Julie had lots of
great ideas for having fun.

She and Minnie ran under the sprinkler in their bathing suits.

They baked yummy
chocolate chip cookies.

They painted pictures and made doll furniture from ice-cream sticks.

On Saturday, Julie and her grandma took Minnie to the beach.
Julie and Minnie had a wonderful time splashing in the waves,
building sandcastles, and collecting pretty shells.

That evening as they rode home, feeling tired and sandy but happy, Minnie saw Daisy skating up and down the sidewalk all alone.

"Oh, no!" Minnie cried. "I promised Daisy I would spend all day today with her — and I forgot! I've got to call her right away!"

The minute Minnie got home, she hurried to call Daisy before she even changed clothes. She stood in her bathing suit and towel, listening to Daisy's phone ring and ring and ring. But Daisy didn't answer. Minnie took a shower, got dressed, and tried calling again. But still no answer! Minnie was very worried!

Just then, Julie knocked on the door. "Grandma says you can sleep over, if you want," she said.

"I don't know," Minnie said. "I'd like to, but I really need to talk to Daisy."

"You can call her from my grandma's house," Julie suggested.

"Okay," Minnie agreed.

Soon she and Julie were snuggled in their sleeping bags with the lights off. They held a flashlight under their chins and made silly faces.

"This is fun," giggled Minnie — so much fun that she forgot to call Daisy!

When Minnie went home the next morning, she found a big brown envelope by her door. Inside it was Daisy's best-friend charm bracelet and a note.

"Dear Minnie," the note read, "I thought we were going to spend yesterday together. I guess I'm not your best friend anymore. Daisy."

Minnie ran over to tell Julie about Daisy's letter and the bracelet.

"Daisy must think you've forgotten about her," Julie said. "I have a best friend, too. I'm braiding this friendship bracelet to send to her so she'll know I'm thinking about her while I'm away."

Minnie thought about what Julie said, then she smiled a great big smile.

"I have an idea!" she exclaimed. "Will you show me how to make friendship bracelets? I'm going to make lots of them for Daisy!"

"Good idea!" said Julie. "I'll help!" Together they made dozens of bracelets in red, yellow, blue, green, and pink — all Daisy's favorite colors.

Minnie looped the bracelets into a long chain, then put them into a pretty blue bowl with pink hearts on it. "Now, let's go see Daisy!" she cried.

Minnie and Julie ran to Daisy's house and knocked on the door.

"Hi, Daisy," Minnie said shyly as she handed her the bowl. "This present is for you."

Daisy was surprised. "A present for me?" she asked. "What is it?"

She looked in the bowl and started to pull out the chain of bracelets. As Daisy pulled bracelet after bracelet from the bowl, she began to smile. Finally, she pulled out the last one! There was her best-friend charm bracelet, tied to the end.

"I'm sorry I hurt your feelings," Minnie said. "I didn't mean to forget you. You'll always be my best friend."

"I'm sorry, too," said Daisy. "I was really jealous of you at first, Julie, but now I'd like to be your new friend, too. Would you teach me to make friendship bracelets?"

"Sure!" Julie exclaimed. She ran home to get her yarn.

Soon Daisy, Minnie, and Julie were sitting on Daisy's porch, sipping lemonade and making brightly-colored bracelets for everyone they knew.

"I'm glad I have *two* nice, new friends," said Julie.

"Here," Daisy said as she finished a friendship bracelet and slipped it over Julie's wrist. "I'm glad we're friends now, too. This is for you to remember me by."

"Thank you!" said Julie. "It's beautiful."

Minnie watched her two friends happily. She held up her arm and looked at her bracelets. "I'll always wear my braided friendship bracelet to remind me of my new friend *and* my best-friend charm bracelet to remind me of my old friend," she said with a smile. "Because it's nice to have both kinds of friends!"

Daisy and I wear our friendship bracelets every day. Have you ever made something special for a best friend?